To ....

From ....

MR. MEN   LITTLE MISS
MR.MEN™ LITTLE MISS™ © THOIP (a SANRIO company)

Mr. Men My Daddy © 2017 THOIP (a SANRIO company)
Printed and published under licence from Price Stern Sloan, Inc., Los Angeles.
Published in Great Britain by Egmont UK Limited
The Yellow Building, 1 Nicholas Road, London, W11 4AN

ISBN 978 1 4052 8644 2

67157/2
Printed in Italy

MIX
Paper from
responsible sources
FSC® C018306
FSC
www.fsc.org

Egmont is passionate about helping to preserve the world's remaining ancient forests.
We only use paper from legal and sustainable forest sources.

This book is made from paper certified by the Forest Stewardship Council® (FSC®),
an organisation dedicated to promoting responsible management of forest resources.
For more information on the FSC, please visit www.fsc.org. To learn more about
Egmont's sustainable paper policy, please visit www.egmont.co.uk/ethical

MY DADDY

by Roger Hargreaves

and me

My daddy is full of fun from the moment he wakes up.

He is as silly as Mr Funny
and can pull the best faces.

My daddy can do the most impossible things.

And sometimes he can even make my dreams come true.

My daddy is as tall
as Mr Tall.

And as strong as Mr Strong.

He is the fastest thing on two legs.

And he can eat the most enormous
plates of food.

My daddy is very clever and knows lots of things.

But he can't always
do everything
he tries.

He reads stories in the loudest, funniest voices.

And I can even hear him
when he's sleeping.

My daddy can sometimes be a bit grumpy, just like me.

But he's always there to help me when I'm tired.

He has a style all of his own.

And sometimes likes things to be just so.

But my daddy is so much fun
and can make anyone smile.

Especially when he tells
his silly jokes.

We do the coolest
things together.

But he also likes a bit of quiet time.

My daddy is full of mischief.

And you have
to watch out
for his tickles.

Life with daddy is one big adventure.

I think he might have even met Father Christmas.

When I'm happy, it makes him happy too.

My daddy is the best daddy
in the whole world.

I love my daddy
and he loves me.

MY DADDY

My daddy is most like **MR.** ....

I love it when my daddy reads ....

.... to me.

My daddy makes me laugh when ....

....

He always knows when ....

....

My daddy is very silly because ....

....

My daddy is lots of fun and likes ....

Our favourite thing to do together is ....

I know he loves me when ....

My daddy's tickles are the best because ....

....

This is a picture
of my daddy:

by ....

aged ....